For
Matilda, Marigold,
and
Skritty Kitty (of course!)

SIMON & SCHUSTER BOOKS FOR YOUNG READERS

An imprint of Simon & Schuster Children's Publishing Division

1230 Avenue of the Americas, New York, New York 10020

Copyright © 2012 by Emily Gravett

Originally published in 2012 in Great Britain by Macmillan Children's Books

First U.S. edition 2014

SIMON & SCHUSTER BOOKS FOR YOUNG READERS is a trademark of Simon & Schuster, Inc.

For information about special discounts for bulk purchases, please contact

Simon & Schuster Special Sales at 1-866-506-1949 or business@simonandschuster.com.

The Simon & Schuster Speakers Bureau can bring authors to your live event. For more information or to book an event,

contact the Simon & Schuster Speakers Bureau at 1-866-248-3049 or visit our website at www.simonspeakers.com.

The text for this book is hand lettered.

The illustrations for this book are rendered in oil-based pencil, watercolor, and colored pencils.

Manufactured in China • 1213 MCM

2 4 6 8 10 9 7 5 3 1

Library of Congress Cataloging-in-Publication Data

Gravett, Emily, author, illustrator.

Matilda's cat / Emily Gravett.—First U.S. edition.

pages cm

First published in Great Britain in 2012 by Macmillan Children's Books, London.

Summary: Illustrations and simple text expose Matilda's attempts to learn what her cat likes best, as well as the real answer.

ISBN 978-1-4424-7527-4 (hardcover)

ISBN 978-1-4424-7528-1 (eBook)

[1. Cats—Fiction.] I. Title.

PZ7.G77577Mat 2013

[E]—dc23

2012049731

Matilda's Cat

Emily Gravett

Simon & Schuster Books for Young Readers
NEW YORK LONDON TORONTO SYDNEY NEW DELHI

Matilda's cat likes
playing with wool,

~~playing with wool,~~
boxes,

~~playing with wool,~~

~~boxes,~~

and riding bikes!

Matilda's cat likes
tea parties,

~~tea parties,~~
funky hats,

~~tea parties,~~
~~funky hats,~~
and fighting foes!

Matilda's cat likes
drawing.

~~drawing,~~

climbing trees,

~~drawing,~~
~~climbing trees,~~
and bedtime stories.

Matilda's cat does NOT like
    playing with wool,
    boxes,
        riding bikes,
        tea parties,
    funky hats,
    fighting foes,
        drawing,
        climbing trees,
OR bedtime stories.

Matilda's cat likes...